TEACHER'S MANUAL FOR
RESUSCITATED

A COVID-19 TRAGEDY

MERRY CHRISTIAN

WestBow Press books may be ordered through booksellers or by contacting:

WestBow Press
A Division of Thomas Nelson & Zondervan
1663 Liberty Drive
Bloomington, IN 47403
www.westbowpress.com
1 (866) 928-1240

Because of the dynamic nature of the Internet, any web addresses or links contained in this book may have changed since publication and may no longer be valid. The views expressed in this work are solely those of the author and do not necessarily reflect the views of the publisher, and the publisher hereby disclaims any responsibility for them.

Any people depicted in stock imagery provided by Getty Images are models, and such images are being used for illustrative purposes only. Certain stock imagery © Getty Images.

All Scripture quotations are taken from the King James Version.

ISBN: 978-1-9736-9428-1 (sc)
ISBN: 978-1-9736-9427-4 (e)

Library of Congress Control Number: 2020911280

Print information available on the last page.

WestBow Press rev. date: 6/30/2020

WESTBOW
PRESS®
A DIVISION OF THOMAS NELSON
& ZONDERVAN

To the teacher:

This comprehensive and intensive study guide on *Resuscitated – A COVID-19 Tragedy* is written to introduce the student to the structure of a novel and the literary techniques that authors use to write their narrative. It is meant to be a companion to the book *Resuscitated – A COVID-19 Tragedy.* Deconstructing literature will increase reading comprehension and instruct indirectly in good writing compositions.

This study guide can be used in any order; however, some sections under "Structural Elements of a Novel" would most easily be completed while reading the novel. Conflict and theme cannot be completed until the entire book is read.

The section "Sound Techniques" can be used anytime and includes a worksheet on identifying alliteration, assonance, and onomatopoeia. Teaching sound techniques first would help a student recognize alliteration, assonance, and onomatopoeia as they read.

Except for the sections on idioms and allusions, the figurative language sections can be completed by chapter 16. The worksheets on idioms, allusions, pseudonym, and literary license are best completed after reading the novel.

Vocabulary exercises have been divided into ten-chapter units. All of the words are in the glossary in the study guide. Some students may need reminded that they should do these vocabulary exercises by the process of elimination. Another hint: the synonyms should match in tense (for verbs) and parts of speech (example: both should be adverbs).

The vocabulary exercises worksheets are in the student study guide. Quizzes and extra credit opportunities are only found in this teacher's manual.

INDEX

GENERATE INTEREST BEFORE THE BOOK!

Using personal experience or by interviewing an adult who lived during the coronavirus pandemic of 2020, students could:

1) write a paragraph(s) describing the COVID-19 pathogen. Discuss and compare the students' descriptions to the author's descriptions in the last two paragraphs of chapter 27.

2) write a narrative about the changes in family life during the COVID-19 pandemic.

3) write a narrative about the adaptations businesses made to continue to operate during the pandemic.

4) explain the changes made in a particular occupation due to the coronavirus.

5) write a compare-and-contrast paper about their schooling before and after the COVID-19 pandemic.

6) describe the charitable deeds done by individuals, organizations, or businesses.

7) describe a visit they have made to a nursing home.

8) interview a patient in a nursing home.

INTRODUCTION TO GENRE

What causes you to read a book? Some readers have a preferable author, and most readers have a preferable **genre.** Genre refers to the style, the form, and the content of the writing. Readers can be drawn to content that interests, informs, and/or entertains them. There are four main genres in literature: poetry, prose, drama, and nonfiction. **Prose** refers to communication that is written using everyday speech. Newspapers, textbooks, and novels are examples of prose. Newspapers, textbooks, and **nonfiction** differ from prose, poetry, and drama in that the first is true or factual. Prose, poetry, and drama are works of **fiction** because they are not entirely true or factual, although there could be many truths or facts within the manuscript.

A **novel** is a long prose composition which is usually published in book form. Most readers narrow their novel choices to favorite **subgenres** such as folklore, mythology, mystery, romance, thriller, diary, historical fiction, science fiction, and realistic fiction.

When selecting a hard copy of a book, whether hardcover or softcover, a reader will be drawn to the book's cover. Hardcover books often have a <u>dust jacket</u>, a removable paper covering with flaps which gives information about the book. The author's photograph and background, the book's summary, and a book excerpt may be some of the information on the dust jacket. These descriptions help a reader to decide if they want to read the book.

Electronic books (eBooks) are marketed using much the same information via technology. Besides searching the database by title or author, searches can be made using key words which match the content of the book. The author's name, the book title, and the keywords are used by libraries and distributors to direct a reader to the book's page. Here the reader will find much the same information about the book that is found on a dust jacket.

After you finish reading *Resuscitated – A COVID-19 Tragedy,* use specifics from the book to explain why the novel is realistic fiction.

> *Resuscitated – A COVID-19 Tragedy* is a work of fiction. Stated on the copyright page at the beginning of the book is this disclaimer - "All of the characters, names, incidents, organizations, and dialogue in this novel are either the products of the author's imagination or are used fictitiously." The novel is realistic fiction because much in the narrative seems as if it could have happened. The book contains accurate information on various subjects, which is woven throughout the narrative. The most obvious, realistic aspect of the novel is its facts on the COVID-19 world-wide pandemic that the United States and the world endured in 2020. Descriptions about the procedures for prison visitations and nursing home visitations are also factual.

THE PLOT

The **plot** is the events or the action of the novel. In a typical story, the plot follows a pattern of introduction, rising action, climax, falling action, and denouement. The **introduction** gives the background information that the reader needs to be able to understand what is about to take place in the story. The **rising action** is the events that create interest and suspense. It is during this part of the novel that a **conflict** is introduced. The point at which this conflict becomes the most exciting or strongest is called the **climax.** The narrative after the climax is the **falling action.** During this part of the story the author will tie up all the loose ends. The part of the story that deals with the resolution or the final outcome of the conflict is the **denouement**

What event do you think is the climax of this novel?

Chapter 21 – the arraignment and imprisonment of Dr. Bush

THE SETTING

The setting of a novel includes **when** and **where** the action occurred. Sometimes the setting is precise; sometimes the setting is vague. Often the reader must gather hints as she reads to determine the "when" and the "where" of a story.

When did *Resuscitated – A COVID-19 Tragedy* did place?   spring 2020 (chapters 1, 23, 26)

Where did *Resuscitated – A COVID-19 Tragedy* take place?   southwestern PA (chapter 23)

POINT OF VIEW

The **point of view** of a novel is the method an author uses to relate the story. One can determine the point of view by asking the question, "Who is telling the story?" If the main character expresses himself or herself using first person pronouns such as I, me, my, and mine, then the point of view is **first person point of view.** If the narrator uses second person pronouns such as you or your, then the story is **second person point of view.** Narratives using third person pronouns such as he and she are in the **third person point of view.** There are two types of third person point of view. One is called third person **limited** point of view when the story is told by a narrator who does not have insights into a character's thoughts. The third person **omniscient** point of view is told by a narrator who knows everything about the characters, including their thoughts. Omniscient means "all knowing" like God who knows everything.

In what point of view is *Resuscitated – A COVID-19 Tragedy* written?

third person omnisctient

CONFLICT

The struggle or challenge in the story that a character faces is called the **conflict.** There may be more than one conflict in a narrative, and different characters may be challenged by different adversaries. Most conflicts or struggles can be categorized as man vs man, man vs nature, or as man vs himself. The first two types of conflict are self-explanatory. The conflict of man vs himself is an inner struggle, a psychological conflict, that the character is trying to answer. Most conflicts are resolved during the denouement of the novel, although some authors leave a conflict unresolved for a **hanging ending** to their book.

Write several paragraphs about the conflict(s), in *Resuscitated – A COVID-19 Tragedy*. For the conflicts(s), name the two opposing forces and use examples to argue whether the author resolved the struggle(s).

> The major conflict in *Resuscitated – A COVID-19 Tragedy* is introduced three times in the first ten paragraphs of the novel. The author, Merry Christian, states that the protagonist, Sarah, wrestles with remorseful and conflicting thoughts. This guilt is caused by a secret (a secondary conflict) which is alluded to numerous times when Sarah refuses to directly answer questions about her miraculous recovery from end-stage cancer. The secret is not completely revealed to the reader until chapter ten.
>
> Not only does loyalty to Dr. Stephen Bush, who resuscitated Sarah, cause the initial conflict, but it also triggers an emotional struggle within Sarah. First, she has to deal with her love for Edna. Sarah's love compels her to ask Stephen for the illegal cancer cure, but Sarah's conscience bothers her in putting Stephen at personal risk.
>
> Throughout the narrative, the reader is given insights into Sarah's thoughts. She feels she has been given a new life and, because of this resuscitation, struggles with herself and others to live a more grateful Christian life in service to others. This man versus himself conflict is never fully resolved, as it can be with no human being, because there are always decisions to be made about priorities in life. By the end of chapter 25, Sarah seems to have come to peace with herself when the author states that Sarah's life was now more fulfilling due to her Christian charity - she had become a Merry Christian.
>
> Dr. Stephen Bush's illegal medical actions precipitated the emotional dilemmas that confronted Sarah and caused his conflict with the government. This latter man-versus-man problem in the story was partially resolved with Stephen's death; however, the reader is left with several remaining questions: What was the medicine that Stephen used to heal his patients? Would this medicine ever be approved by the Federal Drug Administration? Since Stephen had determined that cancer was caused by an "obscure, mutating virus," could his medicine have been a cure for COVID-19? The reader is left with these hanging questions.

HOOKS

A **hook** in literature is a deliberate effort by the writer to initially engage the reader and stimulate them to continue reading. Hooks are found at the beginning of prose and sometimes throughout the composition to continue to motivate the reader to finish the novel. List the two hooks found in chapter 1 of *Resuscitated – A COVID-19 Tragedy*.

> A wave of remorse flooded her soul as she wrestled with her secret.
> Again guilt stabbed at Sarah's heart.

You will find unfinished sentences, questions, or thoughts in *Resuscitated – A COVID-19 Tragedy* that the author has used to keep you hooked in the narrative. As you continue reading *Resuscitated – A COVID-19 Tragedy*, write down any other hooks that you find in the story.

> I know that they will have many questions, and I am not prepared to answer them yet.
> It was the Word and tea that would guide her response to her situation.
> "I think that everyone who cared for me during my war with cancer has been part of my restoration," Sarah tried to say convincingly but sternly changing the subject.
> As a tenant, the harsh clatter had always brought feelings of loss and apprehensive questions of 'Who? When? Who next?' This time her mind wildly asked - Edna?'
> It was Tuesday, and Sarah was looking forward to her visit with Edna, but was wretched and anxious to see Stephen.
> "Hi, Sarah," returned an unfamiliar voice.

FLASHBACK AND FORESHADOW

Both flashbacks and foreshadows are narrative that is out of chronological order in a story. A **flashback** gives the reader information that occurred before the novel began. Flashbacks in the form of dreams or reminisces are often woven into a plot to help the reader understand the characters or the action of the novel. While a flashback happened in the past, a **foreshadow** hints about something that is going to happen in the future in the plot. Foreshadows build suspense, are often very subtle, and may be missed by a reader until the event that had been foreshadowed actually happens.

What flashbacks can you find in *Resuscitated – A COVID-19 Tragedy?*

> Chapter 6 – first six paragraphs
> last paragraph of chapter 9

What foreshadows can you find in *Resuscitated – A COVID-19 Tragedy?*

> As she moved to seat herself on the bench in the foyer, she suddenly realized that it was gone. She wondered why it had been moved.
> What if her grandchildren didn't want to relinquish Shep and Oreo?

4

Continuing the ascent, another premonition shuddered through her being. Why was she nervous?

"As I explained to Jared, Anne, and you, this had to be done secretively; I could not document the medication."

As a tenant, the harsh clatter had always brought feelings of loss and apprehensive questions of 'Who? When? Who next?' This time her mind wildly asked - Edna?'

Chapter 26 – announcement of COVID-19 pandemic

"Well, the peril of medical staff in many places is being recognized with hazard pay."

…a later photo of a mass grave for unclaimed bodies was traumatizing.

"Hi, Sarah," returned an unfamiliar voice.

THEME

All authors write for a purpose; they have an idea to express, a message, or a moral. Like a good joke teller who never explains why his joke is funny, a writer lets his composition speak for itself as to the theme. Short writings often have just one theme, but longer manuscripts may have several themes. When more than one theme is expressed, one is usually the dominant theme or main purpose of the writing.

Write several paragraphs about the theme(s) of *Resuscitated – A COVID-19 Tragedy*. Use specific examples from the story to support your choice of the theme(s). If you argue that the novel has more than one theme, then give textual proofs as to which theme is the dominant theme or the most important idea that the author is trying to convey.

In *Resuscitated – A COVID-19 Tragedy,* the protagonist, Sarah, realizes that her life before being resuscitated from end-stage cancer was not one of Christian service to mankind. Sarah realized that Jesus had promised a resurrection after death, an eternal second life, and she had not shown her gratitude for this promise and the sacrifice that Jesus had made for her. The narrative informs the reader of new choices made by Sarah in her second-chance life and is also replete with examples of the charitable deeds done by others during the COVID-19 pandemic. The author suggests that such a sacrificial life will be more fulfilling and make a person a "Merry Christian." Mentioned three times in the novel, the hymn "A Beautiful Life", becomes Sarah's personal mission statement and encapsulates the main theme of the book. By identifying with Sarah's emotional struggles and decisions, the author wants the reader to question their own priorities in life and make changes as Sarah did. The author seems to conclude as in James 4:17, "Therefore to him that knoweth to do good, and doeth it not, to him it is sin."

Several minor themes in the novel were apparent by their repetition. Three times friends were considered "priceless…precious…matchless." Not only did the three occurrences and the three adjectives emphasize the importance of friends, but the comfort and support given by the minor characters to Sarah in the novel during her stay and after her discharge from the care center was also praised and lovingly related. The Bible admonishes Christians to bear each other's burdens, and these examples of good deeds contribute to the theme of service and sacrifice.

Mentioned only twice but in very emotional situations, the two partings of "see you later," and "goodbye," stressed to the reader the finality of some earthy departures. The "see you later" indicates a meeting of the speaker and the deceased, an afterlife. The author subliminally asks this question of the reader, "What would be your parting words?"

The last minor theme was repeated five times generally as "Life had gone on…as it always had… and as it always would." This truism is comforting in some respects as routine calms and comforts in stressful situations; however, the author does not want the reader to become complacent in that maxim because he finishes that phrase twice with "life does not stop for death." These words remind the reader of James 4:14, "Whereas ye know not what shall be on the morrow. For what is your life? It is even a vapor, that appeareth for a little time, and then vanisheth away."

FIGURATIVE LANGUAGE

When writers use a word or phrase which cannot be taken literally, that is according to the definition(s) of the word(s), then they are using figurative language. The meaning of the word or words used has additional meaning beyond the definitions or may not appear to have any meaning related to the definitions of each word. Readers must be fully engaged to comprehend these figures of speech, as they give nuances and depth to the meaning that the author is trying to convey. There are over one hundred figures of speech. The most common are simile, metaphor, personification, hyperbole, understatement, irony, oxymoron, allusion, and idiom.

SIMILE

Simile is a figure of speech that makes a comparison between two things that are not alike but do share some similarities. These different words or ideas are connected by the word "like" or "as." In the example "teeth as white as milk," the reader knows that both teeth and milk are white, but using this simile emphasizes how really white the teeth are. Another example: Her eyes were like sparkling sapphires.

Find a simile in both chapter one and chapter 6.

> chapter 1 - Like a bullet, the truth pierced her heart- her entire home's contents had been cleared out.
> chapter 6 - …a corner of the unheated, gravel-floored basement had provided the lavatory necessities, but it had been like using an arctic outhouse.

METAPHOR

Metaphor is a simile which compares two things that are not alike but do share some similarities. A metaphor differs from a simile in that the words "like" or "as" are **not** used. "I am the good shepherd" is a metaphor.

Find the metaphor in the opening sentence of *Resuscitated – A COVID-19 Tragedy*.

> cotton-ball clouds

PERSONIFICATION

Personification is a figure of speech that uses human qualities to describe nonhuman things.

We have long personified the natural world as Mother Nature and the United States government as Uncle Sam. **Anthropomorphism** is very similar to personification. In this case, the writer makes an animal or object behave and appear like it is a human being, as in the children's classic *The Little Engine that Could*.

Find as least three examples of personification in chapters 1-3 in *Resuscitated– A COVID-19 Tragedy*.

...center garden was resplendent with fuchsia pinks and sundry-colored bachelor buttons. These volunteers had never so thrilled her heart, and her eyes misted at their exuberant welcome.

... the lilac's annual display and gift

In a daze she passed through to the living room. It also was desolate and forlorn.

Sarah strolled out to sit on the steps of her deck in the company of the embracing, friendly sun.

HYPERBOLE AND UNDERSTATEMENT

Hyperbole is an exaggeration that obviously is not true. Authors use hyperbole to emphasize a thought. Examples: Your purse weighs a ton. The horse broke from the gate faster than a lightning bolt.

Understatement is the antonym of hyperbole. Example: She had lost so much weight that she was light as a feather.

Find the hyperbole in chapter 3 in *Resuscitated– A COVID-19 Tragedy*.

For an eternity, the two women stood staring at each other.

Find the hyperbole in chapter 11.

"Really strong, and stronger as each second goes by," Sarah replied.

IRONY

Irony is using words or developing situations which mean the opposite of what a reader would expect. Situational irony is when the opposite result occurs from what is to be expected.

(example: The police station was robbed of its petty cash.) Verbal irony is saying one thing and meaning the opposite. (example: The assembly instructions were as clear as mud.)

Find the two ironies in chapter 1 of *Resuscitated – A COVID-19 Tragedy*.

Plowed fields brought the fragrance of moist, tilled loam and the remembrance of the aroma of freshly spread manure.

There was so much work to look forward to!

Write an explanatory paragraph about the situational irony in the book's ending.

In life, one expects the old to die before the young. In *Resuscitated – A COVID-19 Tragedy,* not only is this reversed, but there is a two-fold irony in that doctor Stephen dies before patient Sarah. Also, Stephen who developed a medicine to kill an "obscure, mutating virus," dies by an "alien virus."

OXYMORON

Oxymoron is a figure of speech in which two words of opposite meanings are used together. Examples: foolish wisdom; clearly confused

Find two oxymorons in *Resuscitated– A COVID-19 Tragedy,* one in each of chapters 1 and 16.

    chapter 1 – sleepwalk   chapter 16 – open secret

IDIOM

An **idiom** is a phrase that means something different than the definition of the individual words.

The English language is full of idioms, and it is this figure of speech that often gives foreign language persons difficulty when learning English. Idioms are more interesting methods of conveying ideas. Consider these idioms and their meanings.

    That was a blessing in disguise...................something good that seemed bad at first
    Let's call it a day...Let's stop working.

Explain the following idioms (underlined) found in *Resuscitated– A COVID-19 Tragedy*.

    All answers copied from https://www.merriam-webster.com/dictionary.

1.   Chapter 12 "<u>I'll cross that bridge when I come to it</u>. Good-bye," Sarah snapped back and shakily hung up.

    to not worry about a possible problem until it actually happens

2.   Chapter 15 "I try to call when nothing else will interrupt our time together. I'm <u>all ears</u>."

    eagerly listening

3.   Chapter 16 "I think that <u>the cat is out of the bag</u> now."

    to give away a secret

4.   Chapter 28 " I hope that Uncle Sam doesn't defend mandatory tracking by <u>the end justifying the means</u>."

    <u>a desired result is so good or important that any method, even a morally bad one, may be used to achieve it</u>

5.   Chapter 27 "Sarah was determined <u>to soldier on</u>."

    to continue to do something or to try to achieve something even though it is difficult

TO THE TEACHER

At the end of this teacher's manual is an extra-credit worksheet with seven idioms from the book *Resuscitated – A COVID-19 Tragedy*. The following are additional idioms found in the book and can be used as an additional assignment or in classroom discussion. The chapter location of the idiom is in parentheses at the end of the quote.

1. One slow step at a time. (2)

2. I have never heard of anyone coming back from the brink like that. (2)

3. Carefully Sarah analyzed the pros and cons of each dwelling and bounced concerns off her friend Bonnie. (9)

4. I understand that it is a long shot that the kennel may still have Shep. (11)

5. Shep's exuberant, welcome-home greeting for Maria was the nail in the coffin. (13)

6. Tabitha had pulled one over on her! (15)

7. He, like his dad, couldn't carry a tune in a bucket. (21)

8. Now only two residents per table were permitted, a concession which met coronavirus guidelines by a hair. (27)

9. Sarah avoided the depressing newscasts like the plague itself. (29)

10. Jessica was like a fish out of water. (24)

11. I will be happy to keep my cousin in the loop. (24)

12. I know what I said because I felt it was the only goal that might jolt you out of your doldrums. (10)

13. Sarah sobbed as the double whammy pierced her heart and mind. (3)

14. In a fog, Sarah went downstairs and slipped into her shoes. (3)

15. The Bottom Falls Out (title of chapter 26)

ALLUSION

An **allusion** is an indirect, brief reference to something that is widely known about history, culture, or literature. The author assumes that the reader has prior knowledge that would help her understand at what the author was hinting. An allusion adds unwritten information to the text. For instance, in the allusion - Bart was a Solomon in all of his classes.- the reader would expect Bart to be as wise as Solomon. (Note: If a character were named Solomon in a novel and that character was very foolish, then it would be situational irony.)

The following names of characters in *Resuscitated – A COVID-19 Tragedy* are Biblical allusions. Explain the hidden meaning behind each character's name and how that character was like their Biblical namesake.

Stephen

> In the Bible, when the first deacons were appointed to "serve tables," the disciple Stephen was named first; he was also the first Christian martyr in the Bible. Acts 6:8 says, "And Stephen, full of faith and power, did great wonders and miracles among the people." It was the disciple Stephen's zeal to convert and save souls that caused his death by stoning as pronounced by Saul. As Biblical Stephen knew that he was in danger from the ruling Jews, so did Dr.Stephen know that he was at risk for government retribution for trying to save the lives of his three patients in the novel. Dr. Stephen continued courageously, and his three healings were certainly miracles. Faithful to the end, *Resuscitated's* Stephen became a martyr when he volunteered to go to New York to help in the COVID-19 pandemic, and it was the virus that caused his premature death.

Joseph

> The son of Jacob, Biblical Joseph saved his entire family when a famine came to Canaan. Just as Jacob's son took care of his father and brothers, so did Joseph in the novel take care of his mother.

Tabitha

> In Acts 9:36, Tabitha (aka Dorcas) was described as "…this woman was full of good works and almsdeeds which she did." In the novel, Tabitha was the person who had visited Sarah the most frequently in the care center. Tabitha also initiated and planned the welcome-back celebration for Sarah and stayed by her side during difficult and stressful situations. The Tabitha of *Resuscitated-A COVID-19 Tragedy* practiced good works like her namesake.

Herod

> There were six Herods who ruled during the New Testament period. All six ruled with force and were negatively spoken of by the New Testament or historical writers. It is this mean and forceful reputation that is suggested by the author in naming the character in *Resuscitated – A COVID-19 Tragedy* as Herod. It was Herod who argued with and demanded that Sarah have blood tests done.

Explain these other allusions (underlined) in *Resuscitated – A COVID-19 Tragedy*.

1. "It is so reassuring that there are <u>Golden Rule</u> people in the world today."

    the maxim that one should treat other people the way one would like to be treated, often expressed proverbially as "Do unto others as you would have them do unto you." (from Matthew 7:12) copied from https://idioms.thefreedictionary.com/.

2. "Invisible COVID-19 attacked the <u>Titanic</u> sports world."

    The root word *titan* is derived from Greek mythology. The Titans were a race of powerful deities. The adjective *titanic* can now refer to anything extremely large or strong. *The Titanic* was the name of the famous cruise ship that sank in 1912 after hitting an iceberg in the Atlantic Ocean. This name was chosen not only because it was the largest passenger steamship of its time, but also because it was touted as a strong ship, specifically that it was "unsinkable."
    copied from https://www.vocabulary.com/dictionary/titanic

3. "The new normal at grocery stores and other retail outlets mirrored the <u>Draconian</u> measures taken by the Transportation and Security Administration at airports after 9-11."

    Draconian is an adjective meaning great severity, that derives from Draco, an Athenian law scribe under whom small offenses had heavy punishments.
    copied from   https://en.wikipedia.org/wiki/Draconian

4. "The chances of an <u>Orwellian</u> society are becoming more and more tangible."

    "**Orwellian**" is an adjective describing a situation, idea, or societal condition that George Orwell identified (in his book *1984*) as being destructive to the welfare of a free and open society."
    copied from   https://en.wikipedia.org/wiki/Orwellian

5. "These <u>Rosie-the-Riveter</u> classmates worked in isolation but in cooperation."

    Rosie-the-Riveter was a media symbol associated with female defense workers during World War II. These women left their kitchens and made materials for the war effort.

ALLITERATION, ASSONANCE, ONOMATOPOEIA

Alliteration, assonance, and onomatopoeia are writing techniques that use phonetics to embellish and increase the pleasing sound of the script. **Alliteration** is the deliberate and noticeable literary device that repeats identical, initial consonant sounds in adjacent words or two or more words within a phrase. The closer the alliteration is in the text the more effective it is. Tongue twisters are good examples of alliteration as is the term "tongue twister." You are probably familiar with these classic tongue twisters: "Sally sells seashells by the seashore" and "Peter Piper picked a peck of pickled peppers." Not only are alliterations pleasing to the ear, they also can be a mnemonic device. There are alliterative sports teams' names (Philadelphia Phillies), consumer product names (Coca-Coca Classic), and movie and book titles (*Pride and Prejudice*).

There are dozens of alliterations in *Resuscitated – A COVID-19 Tragedy*. Some of these are adjacent words, and some are separated by other words. Examples include: "women stood staring at each other" (chapter 3); "Sarah looked at her watch and waited." (chapter 3); "the bushytails would be bounding beneath the budding trees looking for overlooked, buried acorns from last winter's cache" (chapter 14).

Chapter one of *Resuscitated-A COVID-19 Tragedy* has over two dozen alliterations. List a dozen of them below. Find and circle the alliteration that begins with two different consonants but qualifies as an alliteration because both consonant beginnings have the same sound.

physically feeble but home would facilitate ("ph" and "f" are same consonant sound)
home hearth
weathered the winter
property periodically
gracious those greetings
Community Compassionate Care Center
couldn't calm herself and wanted to cry
father flying
pastures with cattle placidly grazing
never one of her floral favorites but they faithfully brought forth
such scenes had seemed
façade of south-facing windows
dearly departed
depressingly disappointed
thrilling trill
gurgled his gobble
cooing calls
pipping of spring peepers
begrudging bitterness
calming comfort
room-by-room revealed

Assonance is closely related to alliteration and is the repetition of identical or similar vowel sounds in adjacent words or within phrases. Not only are the two tongue twisters examples of alliterations, but they also illustrate assonance. "Peter Piper picked a peck of pickled peppers" repeats the short *i* and the short *e* sounds; "Sally sells seashells beside the seashore" repeats the short *e* sound and the long *e* sound. Assonance differs from rhyme in that rhyme is a repetition of both vowel and consonant sounds. Chapter one of *Resuscitated – A COVID-19 Tragedy* closes with, "Suddenly she felt weak, slid to the carpet, wept, and slept." The ending of this sentence is a rhyme and not an example of assonance.

Find the example of assonance in chapter 1 of *Resuscitated - – A COVID-19 Tragedy*.
   approached her beloved abode

Onomatopoeia is using a word that sounds like the noise that it is representing.

Splish-splash and buzz are examples of onomatopoeia. Find four examples of onomatopoeia in chapter I of *Resuscitated – A COVID-19 Tragedy*.

red-winged blackbirds were already trilling	cooing calls
whacking, thwacking, smacking	rolling burble of robins
whistles of at least three male cardinals	twittering of wrens
strutting turkey gurgled his gobble	pipping of spring peepers

WORKSHEET ON ALLITERATION, ASSONANCE, AND ONOMATOPOEIA

On the line in front of the following excerpts from *Resuscitated – A COVID-19 Tragedy*, identify whether the phrase illustrates alliteration (**AL**), assonance (**AS**), or onomatopoeia (**ON**). Some phrases may be examples of two literary sound techniques.

1. _____ON, AL_____ Somewhere a strutting turkey gurgled his gobble.
2. _____AS, AL_____ pastures with cattle placidly grazing their fenced bounds
3. _____AL_____ The melodious music lifted her spirit.
4. _____AL_____ Edna always beamed and bubbled in their presence.
5. _____AL, AS_____ the debilitating, depressing, and devastating ravages of dementia
6. _____ON, AL_____ the pipping of spring peepers in the wetlands
7. _____AS, AL_____ interrupted her musings as Jeannie maneuvered a wheelchair into the room
8. _____AL_____ drive the rural roads for a country block
9. _____AL_____ to profusely thank everyone for the plethora of pantry foods
10. _____ON_____ Blackbirds were already trilling in her bottomland.
11. _____ON_____ even the soft pitter-patter of raindrops against the windows
12. _____AL, AS_____ Flora and fauna together performed an unforgettable, indelible crescendo.
13. _____AS_____ Daryl would tussle and scuffle with the puppy.
14. _____AL_____ Rewind to fast forward.

15. _____AS_____ Sarah tried to occupy her mind and time.

16. _____ON_____ Oreo yelped a loud meow.

17. ___AL, AS___ after being scanned, searched, and stamped with invisible ink

18. _____AS_____ an approved visitor's list before admittance during visiting hours

19. _____ON_____ She heard the jangling rumble of the steel gurney.

20. _____AL_____ Still a shudder traversed her spine as Stephen's incarceration suddenly became palpable.

LITERARY LICENSE

Literary license is the deliberate act of a writer not following standard grammar, punctuation, and spelling rules. In *Resuscitated – A COVID-19 Tragedy,* Merry Christian made up words, used words incorrectly, and misspelled words. Below are some examples of literary license taken by the author. Read the word in context and explain why you think that the author did not follow formal conventions in her writing.

1. ("Bushytails" is not a real word.)
"It was a warm, cozy day, and Sarah knew that the bushytails would be bounding beneath the budding trees looking for overlooked, buried acorns from last winter's cache."

Using bushytails instead of squirrels makes the sentence more alliterative. With the use of bushytails, there are five *b* sounds in the sentence. Using bushytails instead of squirrels also increases the imagery for the text.

2. ("Purrball" is not a real word.)
In a conscious effort to prolong that comforting dream, and carrying the furry purrball, Sarah arose and methodically visited every nook and cranny of her abode.

Using purrball instead of cat, makes a phrase with assonance and demonstrates onomatopoeia.

3. (The definition of abandonee is: one that holds or claims abandoned property.)
The vow that she had made to visit abandonees at the nursing center was sacrosanct.

Obviously, the author did not use this word correctly, but the writer assumes that the reader knows that the ending "ee" means "a person who is or has _____." Examples include escapee, devotee, and adoptee. Using abandonee emphasizes that there were persons at the nursing center who were abandoned and had no one to visit them.

4. Underline the word or words in these excerpts from the novel that the author has written using literary license. Why do you that think the author used these created words?
" I couldn't control my laughter! I assured Daryl that the growling was <u>puppy-speak</u> for 'Wow! This is great fun!'" Sarah chuckled.
" When Maria asked the employee why Shep kept shaking his head, the girl said it was <u>dog-speak</u> for 'Play with me.'"

Both puppy-speak and dog-speak personify the two animals and make them seem like human companions and playmates.

PSEUDONYM

The term **pseudonym** means "false name" and is also known as a pen name. You are probably familiar with several famous authors who have used pseudonyms. Samuel Clemens wrote under the pen name Mark Twain, and Mary Ann Evans wrote under the pen name George Eliot. The latter adopted a male pseudonym to give her writings a better chance of success, as women writers were not taken seriously in the 1800s. Today a whistleblower may use a pseudonym for obvious reasons.

Do you think that Merry Christian, the author of *Resuscitated – A COVID-19 Tragedy,* is a pen name? Why or why not?

> At the end of chapter 25, the author says that Sarah's life was more fulfilling than before her cancer diagnosis and that now "Sarah was a Merry Christian." Merry Christian has a two-fold meaning. First, "merry" means "happy and cheerful." It seems that at this point in the novel, Sarah is happy and comfortable with the priorities of her life as she tries to be a faithful Christian. This is also a foreshadow of the revelation at the end of chapter 30 when "She started writing
>
> *Resuscitated – A COVID-19 Tragedy"*. Using the pen name Merry Christian fits with and is an extension of the entire theme of the book.

Can you think of any reason for the author to use a pen name to write this book?

> The author may have used the pseudonym Merry Christian to emphasize his theme of the book. When Sarah becomes more committed to God and serving others, her life is more fulfilling; she is happier, that is, she is merry.

GLOSSARY

adieu	goodbye
admonish	rebuke, scold, reprimand
advocate	protector
amble	stroll, ramble
appraise	evaluate
apprise	inform, notify
azure	bright blue
benevolence	kindness, goodness, goodwill
beseech	implore, beg
caveat	stipulation, limitation
chastisement	scolding
compassionate	sympathetic, empathetic, understanding
compulsory	mandatory, required
conflicted	confused
convalesce	recuperate, recover
despondent	discouraged, disheartened, downhearted
disconsolate	unhappy, downcast, dejected
ecstatic	elated, enraptured
empathy	sympathy, understanding, compassion
enigmatic	puzzling
exonerate	absolve, acquit
exuberant	luxuriant, lush; ebullient, enthusiastic, excited
feebly	weakly, frailly, shakily
fervently	passionately, enthusiastically
frailty	weakness, infirmity
hospice	a home providing care for the sick or terminally ill
incarceration	imprisonment, confinement, detention
indelible	ineradicable, unremovable
indictment	accusation, arraignment
infirmity	frailty, weakness
interment	burial, committal, entombment
malevolent	malicious, spiteful, wicked
mandated	ordered, required by law
meditate	contemplate, ponder
melancholy	sadness, downhearted, sorrowful
mitigate	alleviate, lessen, reduce

mortal	perishable
mortality	death, dying
muse	ponder, consider
nostalgic	sentimental
obituary	death notice
obliging	helpful, accommodating, considerate
oncology	study and treatment of tumors
palliative	soothing, comforting, alleviating
palpable	perceptible, noticeable, tangible
passionate	fervent, zealous, intense
pathogen	bacterium, virus, or microorganism that can cause disease
periphery	edge, boundary, border
permeated	saturated, filled
pestilence	plague, epidemic, pandemic
plethora	overabundance
providence	the protective care of God or of nature as a spiritual power
quarantine	isolation, confinement
queried	inquired, questioned
queue	line, file
recuperation	convalescence, recovery
remedial	counteractive, corrective, curative
renaissance	rebirth
resuscitated	revive, resurrect, restore
righteously	rightly, virtuously
sanctuary	refuge, haven, shelter
sojourn	visit, stopover, residence
staccato	series of short, sharply separated sounds
subpoena	summons; a writ ordering a person to attend a court
subtle	indirect
succumb	to die
summons	subpoena, writ, warrant, arraignment
surrogate	substitute
tangible	palpable, real
traumatic	shocking, disturbing, upsetting
vehemence	forcefulness, violence
vindicate	acquit, absolve, clear
vowed	promised, swore

VOCABULARY EXERCISES FOR CHAPTERS 1-10

Below are phrases or sentences from the novel *Resuscitated – A COVID-19 Tragedy.* Within that sentence is a parenthetical word and blank. Study the parenthetical word in context. Select a synonym for the word from the word bank, and write it on the blank line.

goodbye	empathetic	elatedly	understanding	weakly
scolding	passionately	perishable	contemplated	pondered
helpful	fervently	questions	sentimental	comforting
tumor	virtuously	substitute	promised	resided

1. For this (mortal   perishable   ) life, they faced each sunrise without hope.

2. Sarah parked her car and (meditated   contemplated   ) a moment.

3. ... the (obliging   helpful   ) gentleman carried her piece of luggage to the door and bid her adieu.

4. ... the obliging gentleman carried her piece of luggage to the door and bid her (adieu   goodbye   ).

5. Instantly the purring machine would start, and warm, forgiving emotions would overtake Sarah's (chastisement   scolding   ) thoughts.

6. Slowly getting to her feet, Sarah made her way to the stairs and, clutching the handrail, (feebly   weakly   ) navigated to the first floor.

7. They held (nostalgic   sentimental   ) memories for Sarah, but the children may have felt no warm attachment to them.

8. To help us with your perspective, we talked with our parents, for they would be more (empathetic   understanding   ) about you leaving your home.

9. Since your new neighbors have been so (compassionate   empathetic   ) and understanding of my situation, I think that they will fill our shoes easily.

10. Sarah made a cup of tea and again (mused   pondered   ) about the blessed freedom of enjoying a cup of tea anytime she wished.

11. ...these she would always carry with her wherever she (sojourned   resided   ).

12. I prayed (fervently   passionately   ) about it and decided to offer you the treatment.

13. I (vowed   promised   ) that I would work the rest of my life trying to cure cancer and heal other mothers in memory of my mother.

14. You are frustrated because you so (righteously   virtuously   ) and earnestly care for your patients and saving the lives of even strangers.

15. In retrospect I suppose that I was using each of you as a (surrogate   substitute   ) for helping my mom," admitted Stephen.

16. I have been questioned by authorities but have been able to answer (queries   questions   ) rather ambiguously.

17. I will pray unceasingly and (passionately   fervently   ) for you and this complicated state of affairs.

18. Sarah (ecstatically   elatedly   ) grabbed Oreo from Hazel and hugged the furball tight.

19. Think of all the research, drugs, equipment, laboratory tests, doctors' consultations, surgeons' fees, hospital stays, and (palliative   comforting   ) care that my simple pill would abolish.

20. Now after years of successful, thorough (oncology   tumor   ) research, I have determined that cancers are caused by an obscure, mutating virus.

VOCABULARY EXERCISES FOR CHAPTERS 11-20

Below are phrases or sentences from the novel *Resuscitated – A COVID-19 Tragedy.* Within that sentence is a parenthetical word and blank. Study the parenthetical word in context. Select a synonym for the word from the word bank, and write it on the blank line.

protector	stroll	stipulation	required	downcast
confused	dejectedly	enthusiastic	puzzling	recovery
rebirth	summons	upsetting	weakness	ordered
sadness	noticeable	overabundance	filled	edge

1. The medicine of love was escalating her (recuperation   recovery   ).

2. She sat motionless with anger, confusion, and indecision. She must contact Stephen about this (traumatizing   upsetting   ) exchange.

3. Ma'am, do you know that the FDA can get a (subpoena   summons   ) and compel you to submit to this directive?

4. Sarah took the opportunity to profusely thank everyone for the (plethora overabundance   ) of pantry foods that she had found on her doorstep.

5. This plethora of spring (renaissance   rebirth   ) steadied her and levitated her spirits.

6. Sarah positioned herself on the (periphery   edge   ) of the audience that was watching the Girl Scout performance.

7. Yes, I remember when Daryl became (despondent   downcast   ), and I knew that something was bothering him.

8. To lift him out of his (melancholy   sadness   ), I suggested that he go play tug-of-war with the puppy.

9. Looking back over his shoulder and then toward the end of the driveway, it was obvious that the pet was (conflicted   confused   ).

10. Shep's (exuberant   enthusiastic   ), welcome-home greeting for Maria was the nail in the coffin.

11. The last small gift was set before Sarah with an (enigmatic   puzzling   ) caveat from Bonnie attached.

12. The last small gift was set before Sarah with an enigmatic (caveat   stipulation   ) from Bonnie attached.

13. Sarah then and there vowed to be an (advocate   protector   ) henceforth for those imprisoned there.

14. Was today's (frailty   weakness   ) a passing infirmity or was Edna's health on a precipitous, downward spiral?

15. The drizzle had staunched, and the sweet-smelling freshness of new growth (permeated   filled   ) the air.

16. Without a word, Sarah (disconsolately   dejectedly   ) walked the gloomy, cloudy tunnel back to the lobby and out to her car.

17. Joseph had to take one last (amble   stroll   ) around their property.

18. Would she have wanted (compulsory   required   ) visits from her children as a Chinese law mandated in China?

19. Would she have wanted compulsory visits from her children as a Chinese law (mandated ordered) in China?

20. Mid-stride the dog halted and, then with one giant, whining leap, collided with Sarah who by now was kneeling on the pavement with arms outstretched. It was a (palpable   noticeable   ) reunion of love.

VOCABULARY EXERCISES FOR CHAPTERS 21-30

Below are phrases or sentences from the novel *Resuscitated – A COVID-19 Tragedy.* Within that sentence is a parenthetical word and blank. Study the parenthetical word in context. Select a synonym for the word from the word bank, and write it on the blank line.

evaluated	inform	goodness	begging	recuperating
acquitted	refuge	arraignment	isolate	alleviation
microbe	line	revived	indirect	imprisonment
dying	writ	palpable	forcefully	absolve

1. I am certainly going to do everything in my power to have him exonerated," Sarah said (vehemently   forcefully   ).

2. I am certainly going to do everything in my power to have him (exonerated   acquitted   ).

3. She asked God for the strength and the wisdom to do everything in her power to comfort, support, and (vindicate absolve   ) Dr. Bush.

4. Jared and Jessica have received a (summons   writ   ), and it is my understanding that the FDA tried to serve you with a writ on Friday.

5. The righteous indignation which all three felt about their savior's (indictment   arraignment   ) and incarceration was palpable.

6. The righteous indignation which all three felt about their savior's indictment and (incarceration   imprisonment   ) was palpable.

7. Sarah (appraised   evaluated   ) Stephen's handwriting which he had penned on the inmate's portion of the Visitor Information Form.

8. At the announcement for the next visiting group to move to the screening area, Dr. Bush's (resuscitated revived   ) patients complied.

9. Inside a (queue   line   ) formed as signs directed that inmates and visitors would be assigned seating.

10. Stephen was just a number here, but there were some (subtle   indirect   ) differences in treatment.

11. Only minutes later at his appearing did the perception become (tangible   palpable   ) when Stephen entered the room in prisoner's garb.

12. The stark contrast from the purity and (benevolence   goodness   ) of a doctor's white uniform to the shaming, humbling prisoner's uniform shafted Sarah's conscience.

13. While seniors babysat, mothers completed household chores for those (convalescing   recuperating   ) at home.

14. The lawyer did (apprise   inform   ) them of the results of the hair analysis completed by the lab.

15. Being at great danger to (succumbing   dying   ) to COVID-19, Sue's mother could not risk allowing her daughter to quarantine at home.

16. Being at great danger to succumbing to COVID-19, Sue's mother could not risk allowing her daughter to (quarantine   isolate   ) at home.

17. Sarah considered offering Sue (sanctuary   refuge   ) for her self-isolation, but sixty-eight-year-old Sarah was in a vulnerable group herself.

18. I have been catching up on all of the coronavirus information and reading medical reports about this (pathogen   microbe   ).

19. Scientists were using the diagram to reject or endorse (mitigation   alleviation   ) policies proposed by government leaders.

20. The leaders at the epicenter of this pandemic have been (beseeching   begging   ) volunteer medical professionals to come and help them in this crisis.

QUIZ CHAPTERS 1-15, FIGURATIVE LANGUAGE AND ESSAY QUESTIONS

Figures of Speech

Place the number of the figure of speech in the left column on the line in front of its example in the right column.

1.	simile	_____ furry purrball
2.	metaphor	_____ cliff-edge encounter
3.	personification	_____ Herculean effort
4.	hyperbole	_____ like using an arctic outhouse
5.	oxymoron	_____ embracing, friendly sun
6.	idiom	_____ happy tears
7.	onomatopoeia	_____ season's sights and sounds
8.	alliteration	_____ For an eternity, the two women stood staring at each other.
9.	assonance	_____ The birds chirped, the squirrels chattered, and the chipmunks cheeped.
10.	allusion	_____ Shep's exuberant, welcome-home greeting for Maria was the nail in the coffin.

Discussion or Essay Questions

1. In the second sentence of the novel, why did the author refer to Sarah's outside view as "the other world?"

2. Why did the author refer to Sarah's nursing home room as her cell, Sarah's stay there as incarceration, and to Sarah as an inmate or detainee?

3. In your life do you "stop to smell the roses" as evidently Sarah did? Does this idiom refer to smelling flowers? What other things might this idiom refer to besides flowers?

4. Is "call if you need anything" really an offer to help someone or just a perfunctory comment like "have a good day?"

5. Why do you think that Sarah was not allowed to tell anyone of Dr. Bush's treatment of her?

6. How would you describe the Christians in Sarah's church?

7. Do you think that helping someone in time of need is like giving them medicine?

8. What nostalgic memories do you have that give you comfort?

9. Of what was the author trying to remind the reader when he wrote, "When I was thirsty, why didn't you give me something to drink? When I was naked, why didn't you give me some clothes to wear? When

I was imprisoned, why didn't you visit me? When I was sick..,?" Who is Sarah paraphrasing? What was the condemnation that persons received if they didn't feed, clothe, and visit those in need?

10. Sarah's second-chance life has made her reflect on what is important in life. Is what is important in life the same for all persons?

11. Draw a picture of Sarah or describe what she looks like.

12. Could you have agreed to leave your pet with Maria's family?

QUIZ CHAPTERS 1-15, FIGURATIVE LANGUAGE AND ESSAY QUESTIONS

Figures of Speech

Place the number of the figure of speech in the left column on the line in front of its example in the right column.

1.	simile	9	furry purrball
2.	metaphor	2	cliff-edge encounter
3.	personification	10	Herculean effort
4.	hyperbole	1	like using an arctic outhouse
5.	oxymoron	3	embracing, friendly sun
6.	idiom	5	happy tears
7.	onomatopoeia	8	season's sights and sounds
8.	alliteration	4	For an eternity, the two women stood staring at each other.
9.	assonance	7	The birds chirped, the squirrels chattered, and the chipmunks cheeped.
10.	allusion	6	Shep's exuberant, welcome-home greeting for Maria was the nail in the coffin.

Discussion or Essay Questions

1. In the second sentence of the novel, why did the author refer to Sarah's outside view as "the other world?"

2. Why did the author refer to Sarah's nursing home room as her cell, Sarah's stay there as incarceration, and to Sarah as an inmate or detainee?

3. In your life do you "stop to smell the roses" as evidently Sarah did? Does this idiom refer to smelling flowers? What other things might this idiom refer to besides flowers?

4. Is "call if you need anything" really an offer to help someone or just a perfunctory comment like "have a good day?"

5. Why do you think that Sarah was not allowed to tell anyone of Dr. Bush's treatment of her?

6. How would you describe the Christians in Sarah's church?

7. Do you think that helping someone in time of need is like giving them medicine?

8. What nostalgic memories do you have that give you comfort?

9. Of what was the author trying to remind the reader when he wrote "When I was thirsty, why didn't you give me something to drink? When I was naked, why didn't you give me some clothes to wear? When I was imprisoned, why didn't you visit me? When I was sick..,?" Who is Sarah paraphrasing? What was the condemnation that persons received if they didn't feed, clothe, and visit those in need?

10. Sarah's second-chance life has made her reflect on what is important in life. Is what is important in life the same for all persons?

11. Draw a picture of Sarah or describe what she looks like.

12. Could you have agreed to leave your pet with Maria's family?

QUIZ CHAPTERS 16-30, FIGURATIVE LANGUAGE AND ESSAY QUESTIONS

Figures of Speech

Place the number of the figure of speech in the left column on the line in front of its example in the right column.

1.	simile	_____	When was this vile villain going to be vanquished?
2.	metaphor	_____	drew and glued her to the screen
3.	personification	_____	alone together
4.	idiom	_____	gloomy, cloudy tunnel
5.	oxymoron	_____	Dorcas's Legacy Ladies Class
6.	rhyme	_____	ding-dong chimes
7.	alliteration	_____	He, like his dad, couldn't carry a tune in a bucket.
8.	assonance	_____	Sarah moved on only to be sickened and strickened by a sight.
9.	onomatopoeia	_____	It was as if the gurney had silenced all.
10.	allusion	_____	He knew that such a contagion ignited in the prison would spread like a Western wildfire in dry grass and tumbleweed.

1. Are Christians to defend the vulnerable?

2. Why does the author again mention "Life had continued…as it always had…and as it always would"?

3. What was the author trying to infer by using the two partings "see you later" and "good-bye"?

4. What significance might the author have inferred when he named Sarah's home address as Paradise Valley?

5. Why did Sarah and Joseph leave their home at Paradise Valley without looking back?

6. Who do you think God would be more pleased with – a person who sang praises to him out of tune or a person who sang no praises at all?

7. Is it important to you that someone remembers your name and calls you by your name? Discuss some methods people can use to remember the names of other people.

8. Do you enjoy the company of all generations of people? Do you tolerate the different behaviors of different generations? Did Jesus enjoy the company of all ages of people?

9. Have you learned to be content in whatever state that you find yourself?

10. Discuss the incidents in this chapter that give insights into Sarah's character.

11. Is shaming an acceptable and effective method of correcting a person's behavior?

12. During times of emergency, people are willing to give up their freedom for more security. Do you think that we are, or are becoming, an Orwellian society? Could this surveillance eventually be used to persecute Christians?

13. What is the significance to Stephen's death being on Sabbath sundown?

14. Why did Sarah say "good-bye" to Greg but breathed "see you later" to Stephen?

15. Describe what Sarah, Stephen, or Joseph looked like. Pretend that you are drawing a picture of them.

16. How would your life change if you were resuscitated from end-stage cancer?

QUIZ CHAPTERS 16-30, FIGURATIVE LANGUAGE AND ESSAY QUESTIONS

Figures of Speech

Place the number of the figure of speech in the left column on the line in front of its example in the right column.

1.	simile	_7_		When was this vile villain going to be vanquished?
2.	metaphor	_8_		drew and glued her to the screen
3.	personification	_5_		alone together
4.	idiom	_2_		gloomy, cloudy tunnel
5.	oxymoron	_10_		Dorcas's Legacy Ladies Class
6.	rhyme	_9_		ding-dong chimes
7.	alliteration	_4_		He, like his dad, couldn't carry a tune in a bucket.
8.	assonance	_6_		Sarah moved on only to be sickened and strickened by a sight.
9.	onomatopoeia	_3_		It was as if the gurney had silenced all.
10.	allusion	_1_		He knew that such a contagion ignited in the prison would spread like a Western wildfire in dry grass and tumbleweed.

Discussion or Essay Questions

1. Are Christians to defend the vulnerable?

2. Why does the author again mention "Life had continued…as it always had…and as it always would"?

3. What was the author trying to infer by using the two partings, "see you later" and "good-bye"?

4. What significance might the author have inferred when he named Sarah's home address as Paradise Valley?

5. Why did Sarah and Joseph leave their home at Paradise Valley without looking back?

6. Who do you think God would be more pleased with – a person who sang praises to him out of tune or a person who sang no praises at all?

7. Is it important to you that someone remembers your name and calls you by your name? Discuss some methods people can use to remember the names of other people.

8. Do you enjoy the company of all generations of people? Do you tolerate the different behaviors of different generations? Did Jesus enjoy the company of all ages of people?

9. Have you learned to be content in whatever state that you find yourself?

10. Discuss the incidents in chapter 24 that give insights into Sarah's character.

11. Is shaming an acceptable and effective method of correcting a person's behavior?

12. During times of emergency, people are willing to give up their freedom for more security. Do you think that we are, or are becoming, an Orwellian society? Could this surveillance eventually be used to persecute Christians?

13. What is the significance to Stephen's death being on Sabbath sundown?

14. Why did Sarah say "good-bye" to Greg but breathed "see you later" to Stephen?

15. Describe what Sarah, Stephen, or Joseph looked like. Pretend that you are drawing a picture of them.

16. How would your life change if you were resuscitated from end-stage cancer?

EXTRA CREDIT OPPORTUNITY I — EXTENDED METAPHOR

This excerpt from the closing of chapter 27 of *Resuscitated – A COVID-19 Tragedy* is an example of an **extended metaphor,** a comparison of two unlike things continuing (extending) for several sentences or paragraphs. Within this extended metaphor are many other figures of speech. Identify each of the figures of speech. Explain the meaning of any similes, idioms, oxymorons, allusions, personifications, and smaller metaphors in this quotation. Lastly, write a one-sentence summary of the meaning of this extended metaphor.

COVID-19 moved like an invisible, invading army with Pheidippedes' feet and Manticore claws. Like a noxious gas, the coronavirus strangled and suffocated its prey. The Dracula predator siphoned the breath out of its victims. Was the world experiencing God's wrath?

Constantly citizens were reminded by epidemiologists that only they had the power to "flatten the curve", the apex of a hypothetical mathematical graph illustrating the spread and mortality of the pestilence. Scientists were using the diagram to reject or endorse mitigation policies proposed by government leaders. Mankind was facing an invisible, alien killer. The entire world was in uncharted waters. Nowhere was anyone exempt from the grasping, clutching fingers of this slaughterer. Social distancing was considered the linchpin to halt the predator's advance. The world was in this alone together.

EXTRA CREDIT OPPORTUNITY 1 — EXTENDED METAPHOR

This excerpt from the closing of chapter 27 of *Resuscitated – A COVID-19 Tragedy* is an example of an **extended metaphor,** a comparison of two unlike things continuing (extending) for several sentences or paragraphs. Within this extended metaphor are many other figures of speech. Identify each of the figures of speech. Explain the meaning of any similes, idioms, oxymorons, allusions, personifications, or smaller metaphors in this quotation. Lastly, write a one-sentence summary of the meaning of this extended metaphor.

"COVID-19 moved like an invisible, invading army with Pheidippedes' feet and Manticore claws. Like a noxious gas, the coronavirus strangled and suffocated its prey. The Dracula predator siphoned the breath out of its victims. Was the world experiencing God's wrath?

Constantly citizens were reminded by epidemiologists that only they had the power to "flatten the curve", the apex of a hypothetical mathematical graph illustrating the spread and mortality of the pestilence. Scientists were using the diagram to reject or endorse mitigation policies proposed by government leaders. Mankind was facing an invisible, alien killer. The entire world was in uncharted waters. Nowhere was anyone exempt from the grasping, clutching fingers of this slaughterer. Social distancing was considered the linchpin to halt the predator's advance. The world was in this alone together."

allusion:	Pheidippedes	simile:	COVID-19 moved like an army
	Manticore		coronavirus like a noxious gas
idiom:	uncharted waters; linchpin	oxymoron:	alone together
personification:	army, strangled, suffocated, fingers, slaughterer		

In these paragraphs, COVID-19 is personified by using human descriptors: army, strangled, suffocated, fingers, and slaughterer. Attributing human ability to the nonliving coronavirus gives the pathogen almost supernatural power. Comparing the microbe to Dracula imparts breath-sucking images and irrational fear. Such suffocation is magnified by a noxious gas which metaphorically makes the virus invisible, and describing the virus as an alien (killer) adds a frightening unknown to the entire description of COVID-19.

The author uses two allusions in this extended metaphor to add volumes of information about the coronavirus. Pheidippedes was the fastest runner of the army of ancient Greece. He ran from Marathon to Athens without stopping to announce the victory of the battle. After his message was given, Pheidippedes dropped dead from exertion. Like this Greek runner, the author conveys that COVID-19 is a fast, unrelenting, fight-to-the-death army. The virus is also compared to Manticore, an unconquerable mythological creature whose preferred diet was human beings. This tells the reader that COVID-19 is unstoppable and is going to literally consume humans.

The author explains that the world is in uncharted waters, that is the situation is foreign and unfamiliar. The oxymoron alone together tells the reader that everyone must do his own part, but everyone must act together to stop the virus. When the author informs the reader that social distancing was the linchpin to halting the virus, the author uses the idiom to imply that, like the linchpin that holds the wheel on the axle, all mitigation will fall apart without social distancing. If all of the figurative language in these two paragraphs is fully comprehended, then the author has created a terrifying image of the enemy.

EXTRA CREDIT OPPORTUNITY II — ALLEGORY

Resuscitated—A COVID-19 Tragedy is an allegorical novel.

Define **allegory.**

Explain the novel as an allegory.

EXTRA CREDIT OPPORTUNITY II - ALLEGORY

Resuscitated–A COVID-19 Tragedy is an allegorical novel.

Define **allegory.**

Allegory is a <u>figure of speech</u> in which abstract ideas and principles are described in terms of characters, figures, and events. It can be employed in <u>prose</u> and poetry to tell a story with the purpose of teaching or explaining an idea or a principle. The objective of its use is to teach some kind of <u>moral</u> lesson

<u>https://literarydevices.net/allegory/</u>

Explain the novel as an allegory.

In the novel *Resuscitated – A COVID-19 Tragedy,* Sarah is ransomed from earthly death of end-stage cancer by Dr. Stephen Bush who is described as her savior, deliverer, and redeemer. All of the adjectives and the verb "ransomed" used to describe Stephen metaphorically recalls Jesus, our true Savior, who ransoms mankind from a second death, hell. As Stephen physically healed Sarah, so Jesus healed while on earth and was known as the Great Physician. As Stephen resuscitated Sarah, so does Jesus give persons a new life when they become Christians. Sarah shows her gratitude for her healing by dedicating her life to serving Christ, and so should newborn Christians. Stephen's persecution by authorities further recalls the persecution of Jesus by both the ruling Jews and the ruling Romans of his time. Finally, like Jesus, Stephen voluntarily sacrificed his life so that others could live. As Sarah felt compelled to live a more grateful and charitable life in her second chance, so should born-again Christians faithfully serve others, as Jesus commanded.

EXTRA CREDIT OPPORTUNITY III - MOTIF

In literature, a **motif** is a symbolic image or idea that is repeated in the narrative and reinforces the theme or an idea that the author wants to emphasize. Throughout *Resuscitated – A COVID-19 Tragedy,* the author continually uses nouns, adjectives and verbs which are not usually associated with a nursing home or its residents. The words that develop the motif are not used according to the strict definition of each word, but the reader must understand the connotation (the emotional idea) of each word to fully comprehend the hidden meaning that the author is trying to portray. For instance, in *Resuscitated – A COVID-19 Tragedy,* nursing home residents are referred to as inmates. Although the definition of *inmate* includes a person confined to a prison or a hospital, most readers would associate the term *inmate* with the negative confines of a prison. Why did Merry Christian refer to nursing home residents as inmates? Make a list of other words in the novel that develops the same motif, and explain the message that the author is trying to convey.

EXTRA CREDIT OPPORTUNITY III - MOTIF

In literature, a **motif** is a symbolic image or an idea that is repeated in the narrative and reinforces the theme. Throughout *Resuscitated – A COVID-19 Tragedy,* the author continually uses unusual nouns, adjectives, and verbs to describe a nursing home or its residents. The words that develop the motif are not used according to the strict definition of each word, but the reader must understand the connotation (the emotional idea) of each word to fully comprehend the hidden meaning that the author is trying to portray. For instance, in *Resuscitated – A COVID-19 Tragedy,* nursing home residents are referred to as inmates. Although the definition of *inmate* includes a person confined to a prison or a hospital, most readers would associate the term *inmate* with the negative confines of a prison. Why did Merry Christian refer to nursing home residents as inmates? Make a list of other words in the novel that develops the same motif, and explain the message that the author is trying to convey.

Chap. 1 - Sarah glanced around her **cell** of six months.

Chap. 10 - The former **inmate** had gained strength incrementally.
It is so refreshing anytime I can leave this **cell**," Edna said.
I will sign the **release papers** for Jessica tomorrow," Stephen said. (release vs. discharge)
While a **detainee,** she at times had been the recipient of thoughtless, discouraging, negative, and self-absorbed talk.

Chap. 14 - Even with six months of experience as a nursing home **inmate**, Sarah …
Sarah knew that many used these same disagreeable aspects of care facilities as excuses to not visit friends and loved ones **imprisoned** there.

Chap. 16 - Sarah then and there vowed to be an advocate for those **imprisoned** there.
Such community service outreach endeavors had always been savored by Sarah and other **trapped residents**.

Chap.19 - Until her war with cancer and subsequent nursing home **confinement**, Sarah had deluded herself into believing that Jenny cared.

Chap. 21 - Sarah had missed the comforting and edifying hymns while an **inmate** at the nursing center.

Chap. 23 - Her nursing home **confinement** had taught her that one had to make up one's mind to be content wherever they lived.

All of the above underlined terms have negative connotations associated with penitentiaries. The author is subliminally telling readers that, like prisoners, patients in nursing homes lose their freedoms - the freedom of movement and the freedom of choice. For most patients, they do not have the physical ability to leave on their own, and dementia patients are usually locked in so that they cannot wander away. Residents have little choice as to the foods they eat, and they dine, sleep, and bathe when they are told to do so just like prison inmates. In the novel, this loss of freedom is emphasized when Sarah repeatedly muses about the "blessed freedom of enjoying a cup of tea." Prison cells also invoke an imagery of a tiny, living space, a connotation appropriate to nursing home rooms. Using the prison motif, the author is describing nursing homes as unpleasant places in which to live whose residents have lost most of their freedoms. By picturing care centers in such a negative light, the author wants to draw attention to the plight of its residents so that the reader will empathize with residents and visit them. The entire motif is encapsulated with the novel's second sentence: "As Sarah gazed meditatively out her window on **the other world**, she was excited, yet apprehensive, about going home."

Note the use of symbolism in the novel: TEA is a symbol of comfort in the novel; it is not a motif because it is not used to develop the theme. (Tea symbolizing comfort is found in chapters 2,3,5,6,7,11,12,18,21).

EXTRA CREDIT OPPORTUNITY IV - IDIOMS

Underline and then explain the idioms found in these sentences from *Resuscitated – A COVID-19 Tragedy*. The chapter location of the quote is in parentheses.

1. Mankind was facing an invisible, alien killer. The entire world was in uncharted waters. (27)

2. When owners know that they will be passing the baton to another family member, I think they are consummately mindful of their reputation in all of their business aspects. (9)

3. Sarah pledged that she would not return to her old selfish behavior; she would step out of her comfort zone; she would come and encourage those in their final days on this earth. (22)

4. She was determined to maintain the same level of engagement as before COVID-19 reared its ugly head. (27)

5.   It became abundantly clear to Sarah that she would have to make a few notes of the names and her discussions with the new acquaintances, or the next meetings would revert to square one. (22)

6. It was Saturday morning, and Joseph's call came like clockwork. (15)

7. At his quizzical look, Sarah began her narration of her association with Dr. Bush, beginning with their teacher-student relationship through the guinea pig-researcher phase to the triumphal conclusion. (21)

EXTRA CREDIT OPPORTUNITY IV - IDIOMS

Underline then explain the idioms found in these sentences from *Resuscitated – A COVID-19 Tragedy*.

All answers copied from https://www.merriam-webster.com/dictionary.

1. Mankind was facing an invisible, alien killer. The entire world was in <u>uncharted waters</u>. (27)

   new and unknown areas

2. When owners know that they will be <u>passing the baton</u> to another family member, I think they are consummately mindful of their reputation in all of their business aspects. (9)

   to pass job and responsibility on to another

3. Sarah pledged that she would not return to her old selfish behavior; she would <u>step out of her comfort zone</u>; she would come and encourage those in their final days on this earth. (22)

   the level at which one functions with ease and familiarity

4. She was determined to maintain the same level of engagement as before COVID-19 <u>reared its ugly head</u>. (27)

   used to say that something bad appears and causes trouble usually after not occurring for a period of time

5. It became abundantly clear to Sarah that she would have to make a few notes of the names and her discussions with the new acquaintances, or the next meetings would <u>revert to square one</u>. (22)

   the initial stage or starting point

6. It was Saturday morning, and Joseph's call came <u>like clockwork</u>. (15)

    to describe something that happens or works in a regular and exact way

7. At his quizzical look, Sarah began her narration of her association with Dr. Bush, beginning with their teacher-student relationship through the <u>guinea pig</u>-researcher phase to the triumphal conclusion. (21)

    a subject of research, experimentation, or testing

Printed in the United States
By Bookmasters